BOOTLEGGER

by
Brian L. Alvis

Photography by
Robbie Edwards

WORDS MATTER
PUBLISHING
OUR WORDS CHANGE THE WORLD

This book is dedicated to
our Grandparents.

The people I'm going to tell you about in this story are long gone. The winds of Time have blown miles of dirt over their graves. History left them behind, lore and legend never got it correct. This story needs to be told, I'm sure that I am the only one left alive that knows it. All that's left are my memories and some old faded pictures. I don't have much time left, so here is the true story of my family, the Little Rose Gang.

CHAPTER 1

Prohibition officially started on my eighth birthday. I didn't even know what the word meant, let alone the law. The first time I really figured out what it meant was at the town square in Salem, Illinois in 1918. We had dropped off some liquor to friends of Pa's around Kinmundy and Alma in northern Marion County. As we made our way back south through Salem, we saw a bunch of church-going ladies marchin' and carryin' on at the courthouse. We stopped to see what the commotion was and heard them, ladies, preachin' fire and brimstone. They screamed at the crowd and the passersby "Liquor is the devil! Alcohol consumption is Satan himself being invited into your homes!" They marched around the courthouse chanting "Do not let him in! Defy that devil Ladies! Support Prohibition!"

Pa and I sat in the car a long spell while those ladies told their stories. Some of 'em were sad, some of 'em were angry. I thought we sat there way too long, but Pa wanted to hear what they had to say. He listened to every word and even teared up a little during one of the ladies' stories'. I thought it was crazy that we were listening to those women holler about how liquor was the end all evil when we had just dropped off a whole truckload of bootleg whiskey. I asked Pa about it on the way home. I could ask him tough questions, and even if he felt uneasy, he would always answer. As expected he thought a good long while about it before he replied. His response was always well thought out based upon the extra-long pause before his answer. His replies always started the same way, "Well…" Then another long pause before the truth came out, even if you didn't wanna hear it. You were gettin' the truth from Pa.

"Those ladies are right…liquor is the devil…whiskey especially. You gotta know how to tame it, and I know the formula. I know exactly what's in it and I know the exact amount of flame to put to it. I can control that old devil. Yep, he ain't nothin' to me. Some men can't handle him. They let him take over, let him take control. That's when awful things happen when that ol' devil is in control. You gotta know your limit, know your fill line. A man's gotta know when to put the bottle down."

I didn't know much about the devil back then, but I did know that Pa made the finest whiskey in all of Little Egypt. It was as smooth as silk on an ear of corn and packed a punch like Dempsey. Folks called it Gypsy Jack's and when they ran out of it they screamed for more. The taste came from a certain type of wood chips Pa used to soak in the barrels, and the sweetness came from sugar that we got from some famous gangsters. Pa was a master craftsman, and it only took a few months for people from miles around to seek out our family brew.

There was no way Pa alone could keep up with the demand for liquor, so he hired folks from the community to help out with the process. Pa had an old still in the woods near the Jefferson/Marion county line that ran full tilt year round to keep up with demand. The business grew over time, and he had to hire a whole team of people to help run four different locations. At the peak of our business, we could turn out well over a thousand gallons a week. Yep, it was quite the operation, we ran sweet whiskey from Effingham to Cairo and everywhere in between. You could drink Gypsy Jack's river to river, from the Grand Rapids Hotel in the Wabash Valley to Augie Busch's place in Alton.

In some parts of Southern Illinois, they would only serve beer when they ran out of their supply of Gypsy Jack's. It was tried and true, the patrons trusted the product, the buyers trusted my

Pa. In those days, there were all kinds of ways to make home-made liquor, and some folks would use whatever they could find to get stoned. They would filter canned heat through a warsh rag or distill some lethal industrial alcohol to make bathtub gin. You might end up with the jake leg or even worse, you might find yourself in a pine box. Hell, even the government sanctioned the poisoning of liquor to make people cut back, but that only resulted in more deaths. Pa explained it better than anyone could, he pulled out a flask and took a pull as we bounced that ol' Ford down a backroad outside the village of Cartter. Then he spoke some more.

"Those ladies want retribution; they don't want law. It don't matter what they're gonna do in Washington or Springfield. Down here, between the rivers, folks will be drinkin'. Prohibition or not." Another pull off the ol' flask. "If those ladies get their way…well, folks like us will have to get a little smarter and a lot faster."

Pa tilted his head a little, looked over at me, winked and then slammed down on the gas of that suped up ol' Ford. The rattling and the whir of the engine kept the rhythm as we sang "Little Brown Jug" the rest of the way home.

Later that evening I got to thinkin' about what Pa had said. It seemed to me that an awful lot of people wanted to tell other people they couldn't drink no more. Listenin' to those ladies' stories did make me think about all the terrible things that can happen when that ol' devil does take over. I'd seen my fair share of drunks even at that young age. I'd seen 'em fight. I'd seen 'em shoot each other over nonsense.

Little Egypt could be a deadly place if you didn't watch yourself. You could end up on the wrong end of a political debate and all of a sudden you're on the hot end of a gun. Most of the violence was fueled by liquor, that ol' devil. I really did understand their point I guess, but then I thought about all the people that rely on liquor as their business, like my family. I thought about the bartenders, the serving girls, the musicians that played late into the night. They would all be out of work. I couldn't see why a deal couldn't be struck or maybe stricter laws, but to outlaw it altogether didn't seem right. Those politicians, preachers, and ladies didn't realize they were creating a whole new problem.

The tornado of crime and violence that swept through Southern Illinois in the twenties has been told and retold. Everyone has heard the stories of the infamous Charlie Birger and the notorious Shelton brothers, but the corner of Little Egypt I grew up in had different types of bootleggers. My father, Jack Monroe made whiskey and helping him was our family business. My Aunt Rose along with my cousins Clairie and Lily were known as the Little Rose Gang. We are unknown to historians, so I'm here to make sure we are remembered. My name is Owen Monroe, and the stories I can tell from prohibition era Southern Illinois have never been told.

Chapter 2

The term comes from sailors in England trying to sneak li-quor aboard the King's ships in their tall black boots. I'm sure there were men with flasks in their boots for as long as there have been boots so no telling when it was first used. A bootleg-ger is someone who is trying to smuggle somethin' into a place where it's not allowed. During prohibition, the term was used by the authorities to describe people like my family. We got lumped in with all the real criminals, the people who ran whiskey but also took part in robberies and murders. We were only criminals in the government's eyes, to the community that surrounded us; we were heroes.

Illegal activities were the daily routine for my family, we weren't trying to break the law, it's just what we did. We sold bootleg liquor years before prohibition started, enough to flood the valleys of Little Egypt. The land between the rivers might have been the wettest place in America during that time. The hills and hollers of the Shawnee forest were just right for hidin' a still. There were thousands of creeks and runoffs that could be used to run a still, and the backwoods folk took advantage. That wasn't the only liquor being poured into the state, no sir, like the rain in a hurricane, it came from every direction. There was rum from the Caribbean, whiskey from Canada and of course everybody knew somebody who made moonshine. There were bootleggers and gangsters from all over that flocked to Illinois.

The government was ill prepared to deal with the crime that came along with prohibition. They trashed our stills, poisoned our whiskey and tried like hell to put my family members in jail but we kept on findin' a way to slip out of trouble. That's why history left us behind, there is little record of our existence. There are hardly any police records or court documents that exist to prove that we were bootleggers. We did have a run in with the law a time or two, but it didn't turn out the way the authorities wanted.

The local Sherriff called us gypsies because of our background, but my family lived in a tiny village for many years. The beginning of the Little Rose Gang began in the southwestern corner of Marion County. Haines Township, just outside of Kell on the Marion/Jefferson county line. Pa and my mother had a little house there with several acres that they farmed with the help of a couple of local boys. I don't have any memories of my Mother; she left just after my first birthday. All I know is that she was a real gypsy, just like her mother before that and well…everyone knows that gypsies don't stay in one place for long. The woman that raised me lived just down the road on a small farm of her own.

Angelina Marie Ruzicka was the name on her birth certificate, but everyone called her Rose. Well, not everyone, some folks called her Little Rose or The Rose, but to me, she was Aunt Rose. She was born in Williamson County in the 1860s, and her mother was supposedly a mean drunk. So, Rose was sent to live with her gangster father in Chicago when she was just a little tike. Sometime in the 1880s, she moved back to Southern Illinois. She and Pa hadn't seen each other in years, so when she first showed up at the farm, Pa was reluctant to take her in. Rose stayed in the brothel at Stickerbush for a few days before Pa found out where she was. He went there in the middle of the night to get Aunt Rose and her two daughters, Clairie and Lily. They lived with Pa and my gypsy mother for a few months until the farm down the road went up for sale. Pa gave Rose the money for the down payment so she and the girls could move in.

Not long after they got settled in is when my mother started leaving for weeks at a time. She would stay at the gypsy camp for a bit and then she would return to Pa. This went on for a couple of years until one day, during a spell when she had been home for several months, she told Pa she was pregnant and it was gonna be a little boy. He always said that since she was with child, he thought she might settle down, but that turned out not to be true. She returned to the gypsy camp, and that's where I was born. A few days later she brought me to the farm and stayed with us for a year before she was gone again but this time for good. Aunt Rose immediately stepped into the role as my Ma, having already been taking care of me. Although as time would tell, she had some of the same tendencies as my mother.

When I wasn't with Pa, I was with my cousins. You see, Aunt Rose would sometimes disappear for spells or she would be laid up for days. So my cousins would take the reins, they fed me, clothed me and schooled me. After a bit, Rose would be back and ready to teach me something new or take me on a new adventure.

As I got older, I spent more and more time with Clairie and Lily as my Pa was makin' and runnin' whiskey while Rose was drinkin' and hangin' out in the local roadhouses. She had found out that Pa made the best homemade whiskey in the county, so a few weeks after my mother left they started sellin' to the neighbors and then to their neighbors. Before long farmers were comin' from other counties to get Gypsy Jack's. Pa had to hire a couple more fellas to help him run another still. Aunt Rose was good for business, and that's why the early name for our small, tight-knit family stuck.

Rose was the type of gal that knew everyone, and they all adored her. She could sing and dance, drink with the men. Rumor had it that she was a showgirl in her younger days. She always told the story of how she had wooed a young Al Capone and took him for some money. A sneaky fox she was, and that's what made everyone love her. The quality of the whiskey and the charisma of my Aunt made for an easy sell in those parts. Lots of folks made their own wine, even Aunt Rose had her own homemade recipe, but none of it drowned your thirst like Gypsy Jack's.

There was a common belief in the area, wine and rum would get you zozzled, but if you were looking to "set a fire," as Rose was known to say, then you wanted what Pa was brewin'. Right before prohibition began, my family was known in several counties. They distributed to certain farms and feed stores where families in the rural areas would come to buy Gypsy Jack's. It was a slick way of doing business because only a handful of people ever saw my Father or Aunt. They used a secret signal to let everyone know where to come get their liquor. If the farmhouse had a rose bush planted on the east side by a window, then that was a place you could buy Gypsy Jack's. Aunt Rose would plant the bushes herself. Even before I was born, there were stories about the "Little Rose Gang" which consisted of Pa, Aunt Rose and her two daughters plus the two farmhands, Gus Nelson and George Williams. When they did pass other cars on the road, none of them even thought that those nice folks had just dropped off a load of bootleg whiskey.

CHAPTER 3

Those bible-thumpin' ladies I was talkin' bout, well they made enough noise to raise the dead and just like flies to a horse pie the preachers and politicians made that their dinner. It sounded like a hornswoggle to me, but the law was passed. Prohibition went into effect in January of 1920 but believe me, that didn't stop the liquor from flowing. That law only made the fires under the stills hotter, the cars faster and the bootleggers braver. In the year leadin' up to the start of prohibition, you could smell the whiskey on the wind as everyone tried to stockpile as much as they could.

Our family operation took a hit that year when the girls went off to pursue their interests outside family activities. The girls had differing attitudes when it came to the liquor and bootleg-

gin'. Clairie would jump right in, help Pa with the still or get behind the wheel and haul that hooch wherever it needed to go. She was a get it done type of gal and Pa really relied on her a lot to "carry the load" sort of speak. Production slowed a bit, and business wasn't so good when Clairie went away to college in Champaign. When she wasn't helpin' us, she substituted at the Little Prairie school when Mrs. Hickey couldn't be there, so it was just natural for her to make a career of it. Clairie was smart, and a live wire. She would have those kids so wound up that they didn't even know they were learnin' but they soaked it up like the sun, and they all sure did love her.

Everyone loved and respected Clairie but Lily, well everyone thought Lily was the jewel of Little Egypt. She was a dreamer and a doer, once her mind was set on something, there was no talkin' her out of it. Lily Jean might have been the stubbornest person I ever met. She refused to help out in the operation in any way

in the beginning. She didn't approve of Rose's drinkin', but she understood that the family made a livin' off of Gypsy Jack's.

So she decided that she would ride shotgun with Clairie as the gunman on liquor runs. It was quite a sight back then to see two young girls rolling down a backroad in the old farm truck. The police wouldn't stop 'em because it was considered inconsiderate to stop ladies by themselves. The cars passing by didn't have a clue about what was stashed inside and what was behind those pretty smiles.

The girls were like spun rope, close as two people can be. When Clairie left for up north Lily went to St. Louis to act in a play at a new theater called the Muny. They gave her a standin' ovation, and the papers even gave her a nice write-up cuz' she was so

good. Years earlier in middle school, a teacher had heard her sing once in the schoolyard. That teacher gave her singing lessons twice a week for months. Then one summer she took Lily across the river to see a real musical, and she was hooked. For the rest of her childhood Lily would go back and forth from lil' ol' Marion County to the big city. She bought a cameo ring after that first show, and she wore it to remind her of that special teacher. With Clairie being gone this time Lily stayed in St. Louis off and on for a few years. She was always busy and got roles in many more plays. I remember her singing some of the songs from those operettas, I didn't understand 'em, but they sure were pretty.

I had to grow up quick when the girls left, so I stuck to Pa like a shadow during that time. I went on all his liquor runs and went with him to check on all the stills. It was a bit dangerous, but I was already a pretty good shot by that time, and there was always a pistol within reach. Pa would carry a pocket full of cash in case we did run across some lawmen, but that also made us a target for bandits. We avoided certain areas where we knew our services weren't appreciated and no amount of booze or money could buy some folks. There was a couple of times that we got caught on the wrong end of some rifles. Pa would always give em the cash, and that was usually the end of it.

Although there was one time, a group of temperance folks cornered us on a back road. They smashed the whiskey, and for a moment it looked like we might not get away with our lives. They told us that we couldn't buy them off, but after much debate between 'em, they took the money anyway. Pa said as we drove away that he was pretty sure they were KKK. The hooded buffoons had attached their wagon to the prohibition movement also. He said, "I can guarantee that their intentions had nothin' to do with liquor and I guarantee that's not the last run-in we have with 'em."

Pa and I kept busy runnin' the back roads when my cousins were gone, but while they were away, Aunt Rose's drunken antics became routine and outrageous. She was wilder than a peach orchard boar, and she ran with some of the legendary characters from Southern Illinois history. She knew the Shelton brothers from her younger days in Little Egypt and introduced them to Pa. He made a deal with them for cases of Gypsy Jack's in exchange for the sugar that sweetened his brew. The notorious brothers had no shortage of rum, but some of their customers had a taste for Pa's special potion.

Pa uncovered some interesting information about his sister from his relationship with Big Carl and his family. There was a certain mystery that Aunt Rose had never revealed to anyone since she showed up on the farm. No one knew who Clairie and Lily's fathers were. All we knew is that they were different men from further down in Little Egypt. One night over drinks and cards Pa found out why Rose didn't talk about it.

Years earlier there was a long-standing feud in Williamson, and the surrounding counties called the Bloody Vendetta. Over the years, what started as a dispute between two families boiled over into an all-out war. The community started choosing sides, and the feud touched almost every household in several counties.

Generations of families fought this war, and some say that the bad blood still remains to this day. By no fault of her own, my Aunt Rose had managed to get pregnant by two men from families on opposite sides of the Vendetta. Folks took this as a serious disrespect, and as should be, there was a lot of bloodshed from that feud. That's why Rose had showed up at Pa's farm, she had been exiled from the community in those southern counties. She thought she could get a fresh start a little farther north.

Chapter 4

There was a lot of chaos goin' on down south that was tearing those communities apart. The criminals had the run of things, and the bootleggin' led to bloodshed in buckets. In our little corner of the world, things ran a lot smoother. That's why I don't like usin' the word "gang." My family was never a gang, we were a family, and we treated our neighbors and friends like family too. We helped each other, looked out for each other and protected each other when we had to. I could tell you countless stories of how our community came together in times of crisis. Hell, the flu in the winter of 1918 bout took me, Aunt Rose and half the county to an early grave. Clairie and Lily sat by our bedside for days until I was better and then went door to door doing check-ins on all the neighbors. Local docs and midwives did their best to keep up, but they were overwhelmed by the amount and severity of the sickness. My cousins, who remained healthy, became heroes in a time of great need.

Pots stayed full of soup, households continued to function thanks to the efforts of Clairie, Lily and their childhood friend Bernice who was a local midwife. She had learned the natural ways of healin' from an old Cherokee medicine woman who healed the sick in those parts for many years. She had died just before the outbreak, and some say that if she were alive when it happened, hardly anyone in this region would have fallen ill. I don't know if that's true or not but I know one thing. My cousins and Bernie were exposed dozens of times to the deadly disease, but by some supernatural power, they never got sick. Nobody wrote articles about it, nobody handed out awards at the end of it. They just did what had to be done to help the community survive, plain and simple. The girls were regarded as saints after that and from that point on, they could do no wrong.

The community helped protect our family and most were willing to look past Rose's raucous ways to help the rest of us. The people around us made sure no harm came to us from lawmen or otherwise. That's also the reason why our family's story never got told, we didn't drop homemade bombs on our rivals, and we didn't make rolling tank trucks.

We worked with the community to provide a service, granted that service was illegal, but demand dictates supply. Violence and death make for great headlines but a community working together to take care of each other and maybe get a little zozzled along the way. Well, that don't sell many papers.

The Little Rose gang managed to stay out of the news for the most part. The main focus of the media and law enforcement in the early years of prohibition was in Williamson, Saline and Jackson counties where the blood flowed like the rivers that surrounded it. Our little operation was just a ripple in the waves of liquor that were crashing on the shores of Little Egypt. Rose did manage to get herself a public intoxication arrest for dancing on a bar top in Salem. Her behavior was legendary in some of the backwoods saloons, but there were places where her gypsy blood didn't take long to wear out its welcome.

Pa picked up Rose from the Marion County jail and made a deal with her. If she would stay out of the places that she wasn't welcome, then he would help her build some little backwoods place of her own. Well, this was a deal that she couldn't pass up, so we cut a path from behind the chicken coup through the woods a few hundred yards. We finished in the spring of 1923, and we built a three-room cabin out back of Rose's farmhouse. The rooms were in a line so walkin' down the path it looked like a small shack only 20 or 30-foot-wide, but it was actually more than 40 yards long with small porches tacked on the front and back.

The front room was cozy with a fireplace and a living area. The door in the northeast corner of that room led to a kitchen area with storage for dry goods on the opposite side. At the back of that room was a closet with hanging coats on one side and a wall on the other with a small square hole in it. That hole was just wide enough to get a gun barrel through. If you made it to the next door, it led to a huge gaming room with a few card tables, a snooker table and a bar that ran the length of the east wall. Some of the pictures you see in this book used to hang on the wall there behind the bar. Beneath the wooden floor, there was an entrance to a cellar that only a few people knew about. You had to take off the fake panels and underneath was a slab of concrete. There was a tiny slit on one side of the slab and a crowbar that hung underneath the bar top. You would pry open the concrete door and climb down a wooden ladder into the cellar. It was cool, dark and had a main room with a light hangin' in the middle. Off to the west was a side room where late night, high stakes poker games would take place. I would deliver drinks from the bar to the hidden room when these would happen.

There were plenty of armed men guardin' those games and for good reason. I saw piles of money in the middle of that table that would make Rockefeller jealous. On the east side of the main room were huge, wooden sliding doors. Behind those doors was somethin' more valuable than any amount of money ever thrown on a card table. Rows and rows of oak barrels full of Gypsy Jack's sweet whiskey. There were only a few sets of eyes that ever saw the inside of that room. Pa made sure that those iron bolts stayed locked and only the inner circle of our family knew where the key was hidden. An army of Pete's and Nuck's couldn't get into that room without an armload of dynamite.

In the early days at Rose's, you could find the laundry list of Southern Illinois' various criminals that would pass through at one time or another. I already mentioned that the Shelton brothers had made a deal with us, but Charlie Birger had an even closer relationship with our family. The Birger Gang made a few appearances at Rose's over the years to throw some cards and stock up on as much of Uncle Jack's as they could get their hands on.

The first couple of times they came around they just played cards and got drunk. Then one day when they came rolling up for a night of hijinx, they passed Lily walkin' up the path from the shack to the farmhouse. As I was watchin', it seemed as though the whole car turned around as every neck bent to look at Lily Jean. The driver even forgot he was operatin' the wheel cuz' he bout ran straight into the front of the cabin. If I hadn't yelled "Hey! Watch it mister!" he might of put that Chrysler in the front room.

I came to find out later that the driver was Connie Newman, one of Charlie's closest cohorts. From that day forth he lost out of every card game as quick as a beagle on a rabbit and was off to chase down Lily to bend her ear.

He quickly found out that she was the quickest hare in the briar patch and there wasn't no catchin' her. Just like any ol' hound dog, he kept tryin'. He bought tickets to her plays and even escorted her around St. Louis while she was there. Lily didn't mind the gangster's company, but he could never win over her heart.

That victory had been decided long ago, and the victor was Augustus Nelson. We called him Gus, and he had a smile that could charm the quills off a porcupine. Gus was hired by Pa when he was a kid, and he started out by keeping up with the farm while Pa tended the stills. Over time he became quite the brewer and bootlegger himself. The one thing Gus could do better than anyone was drive fast. When Pa needed a

delivery to get there in a hurry, he would get Gus to fire up the coupe. There was no stoppin' him once he was pointed in a certain direction. He would go up, over, around any which way to get whiskey to our customers and he would do it fast. Lily rode along with Gus many times over the years, and they formed a close bond. They would have gotten married I suspect, but Lily cared more about theater than she did being a housewife.

Lily wasn't the only one who had an admirer in the Birger gang, Clairie had grabbed the attention of the most famous member of the gang, Charlie himself. They met at a summertime card game in Harrisburg and quickly became friends. Charlie liked the fact that Clairie didn't treat him like the feared gangster that he was. She treated him like he was one of her misguided students. She wasn't afraid to scold him or tell him when he was being unreasonable.

I remember one game in particular that Clairie caught Charlie cheatin' at cards. I'm pretty sure he was doin' it as a joke more than tryin' to win, but Clairie didn't take it so lightly. For a moment it became a little too tense and had to simmer some pots that were boilin'. In those early days, we got to see the fun-loving side of Charlie. Unfortunately for some who crossed his path over the years, the outcome was far different.

CHAPTER 5

Charlie was always helpin' us out in one way or another to win favor with Clairie. In the beginning of 1924, Charlie gave us a little inside information that might have just saved our business and maybe our lives. During that time the infamous lawman, S. Glenn Young was cooperating with those backward boys from the Ku Klux to conduct raids on stills and bootlegging operations all over the southern counties. Some of the raids had turned deadly and angered not only the bootleggers but also the community. We were fortunate enough to not have to deal with the murderous lawman, but we did encounter some locals who thought they could imitate Young's antics.

We had to protect our stills round the clock from foolish people who thought they could stop Pa from brewin'. We paid good money to be on watch and even did it ourselves when we had to.

I spent many nights in a little shack next to the stills. I would stay up as late as I could, but Pa would stay up for days on just a few hours of sleep when he had to.

We first had trouble with the local hoods at the still near Papertown. It was hidden way back in the deep, deep woods and sat at the mouth of a small cave. Huge slanted rocks surrounded the creek and kept it naturally hidden from most people. I always felt safe spending the night at that particular still because you could walk right by it and never know it was there. If you had found it, you were looking awfully hard, or you had followed us out there.

That's exactly what happened when five white hoods appeared from behind the trees one afternoon. They had followed Gus as he was comin' out to relieve us after Pa and I had been there for a few days. All five of 'em wore bib overalls with their hoods and carried either a shotgun or a rifle. I was shakin' like a long-tailed cat in a room full of rockin' chairs as they held us at gunpoint and busted seven barrels of whiskey that were gettin' ready to be delivered. They also blew up the still and the shack with dynamite. Luckily, they didn't have killin' on their mind that day, but they did leave us stranded in the woods when they popped the tires on the coupe before they drove off. Pa knew the property owner, so we walked to his farmhouse and called the girls to come get us. Pa said that we could build another still in a different location and from now on we had to be more careful. The times of payin' people off were over, and it was time to duck and cover. We tried to stay in the shadows and only run deliveries at night from then on.

That surprise in the woods was just some of the same old troubles we had with the white hoods. They were a ragtag bunch, half of them drunks themselves and they could only manage to organize once in a while. They were more of an annoyance then they were a real threat. They would buzz around a bit and then we would have to slap them away. The spring before they had come in the middle of the night and chopped down the trees in Rose's orchard. She grew peaches, apples, and grapes to make her legendary wine but the tolerance folk chopped down darn near every fruit tree in Little Egypt during prohibition. Rose was fightin' mad, and Pa had to stop her from drivin' into town to go cussin' some folks. That winter those hoods gave us a good reason, so we decided to put a stop to their nonsense once and for all.

One chilly February night while we were all out back at Rose's, the still night air was split by sudden gunshots. We all stopped what we were doin' and listened. I was in the game room when I heard the shots ring out and froze like a scared rabbit. Moments later there were more gunshots, and we realized that someone was shootin' at the farmhouse. Pa grabbed the shotgun from behind the bar and let out for the house. He yelled for Gus to follow him and he told George to look after us as he ran out the back door. Lily went to the front room and grabbed the pistol from the fireplace mantle and Rose, being Rose ran to the bar for a drink. I went to the closet where Pa kept the .22 and jumped behind the bar with Rose.

We waited there for a good long hour before Pa came back and told us it was clear. He said they shot up the farmhouse pretty good, but there were no clues as to who it was. We spent a sleepless night at Rose's while Pa and the guys watched for any more shooters. At daybreak, Pa sent Gus to find out what he could from the neighbors, but no one else had any trouble that night. Gus had seen some hoof prints that left the road and went through the field about a mile down the road. Later that night Pa and Gus followed them tracks and were real tight-lipped about what they found.

We spent the next couple of nights holed up at Rose's and hired a few lookouts to keep an eye on any suspicious vehicles in the area. Those were tense days and nights, but my nerves were calmed a little by the arrival of Clairie. She left Champaign as soon as she heard the news and paid one of the baseball players she knew at her school to drive her down south. She was steely silent when she first got home and told us all that she had a plan.

Not long after Clairie got home, we got a visit from Charlie. He had a stranger with him when they came over, and he said that the stranger was a local klansman. He looked a little worse for the wear and most likely Charlie's boys had given him a pretty good beatin' not long before their visit. They took him out back and down the path to Rose's. I was told to stay up at the house, but as usual, I found a way to overhear his sordid story.

According to our bloodied new friend, the local klan had more plans to shut down our little operation. They were going to come after Rose's next. Their plans were to burn it to the ground and put an end to our family's livelihood. Well, this got everyone in the room's blood to boil, and I found out something that day. My cousin Clairie had another side to her that I didn't know about. She went mad with anger and said things to that man that I dare not repeat, even now as an old man.

Clairie screamed in his face with fire, fury, spit and made damn sure that he knew they would not be intimidated by some backward, small-time klansmen. I had never seen Clairie act like that. She was a force of nature that cut through the tension like a quill in a tornado. She instilled fear into the hearts of grown men in the room and from that day forth I saw her in a different light. She would command a new respect from everyone she met. When it came to family, Clairie would be the first line of defense, and if the klan wanted a war, then she would be the General.

Charlie and his boys took our friend away into the night. I'm honestly not sure what happened to him, but we never saw or heard from that man again. Pa, Gus, and George immediately headed out to the nearest still to set some traps. Clairie offered that baseball player double what she paid him to bring her home to stay and give us a hand. After witnessing the interrogation he had just seen, he dare not say no.

Lily told him that he must be "Bats." Then Clairie gave him a good long look and told him, "Now you are." So that's what we called him from that point on. I don't recall ever learning his real name.

Well, we got to workin' on Clairie's plan right quick. Lily and Rose had been cleaning up the farmhouse, so I went up to help them board up windows. Pa told some of the guys to start gatherin' and choppin' wood, and he told Gus to go get as much gas as he could haul. Clairie told us all that night as we holed up, "We won't know when they're coming but you be damn sure they are. When they do, we gonna set a fire."

We waited for two days and nights with no sign of anyone. On the third day Charlie, Connie, and a few others showed up to bring some real firepower. Turns out it was a good thing they did because that night Clairie turned out to be right. They hit the farmhouse first, shot it up again and then they started down the long path to Rose's. The hoods on horseback came first with their white cloth shinin' and their torches lit. As they approached, they saw a giant pyramid of deadwood piled in front of the cabin. They lined up in front of it having no idea why it was there or where we were hiding. A couple of cars approached slowly, and the hoods rode back down the path a few paces to find out what to do next.

That turned out to be their mistake.

When they turned their backs, Clairie and Lily stepped out the front door of Rose's and lit that deadwood with two Molotov cocktails. It shot up quick, higher than the top of Rose's shack and whistled like a teapot from hell. At the same time, Gus and Bats stepped out of the woods and lit the gasoline trails we had made down each side of the path. It raced past the klansmen and set each side of the woods ablaze. The two coupes came to a stop while the horses reared and took a moment to get under control. When they finally came to a calm, there was a moment where all you could hear was the fire roaring and the wood whistling. Everyone seemed to pause for a moment, the hooded riders, the men that had stepped out of the cars. They just looked around wondering how they became trapped by flames. I will say, as scared as I was that I might not make it out of there alive, it was quite an amazing sight. From my vantage point, I could see Pa, and he was just as calm as could be. With a slight wave of his hand, he told me to take better cover because he knew what was comin' next.

The intruders quickly realized that there was only one way out of their situation, so they aimed their barrels and unloaded their Tommy guns into Rose's front room. The hoods on horseback fired their rifles into the woods on both sides of the cabin hoping we were hiding there. Then there was only the whistle of the raging fire again as they stopped to reload and assess the damage. During that pause is when a cold night wind whipped the top of those flames from the giant pyramid. Right then is when Pa and George popped up from their hidin' spot on the roof with their shotguns.

They sprayed the hoods on horseback with buckshot knockin' a couple of 'em from their saddles. The horses turned hightail and ran back down the path to the farmhouse followed closely by the remaining white hoods. As soon as they passed by the cars, that's when Charlie and Connie came out of the side woods with Tommy guns of their own. They disabled both vehicles and quickly got all the thugs to throw down their guns and run or burn to death. They lit out across the field as if their feet were on fire and their hind end was catchin'. As they ran, Gus and I drove the water tanker that Charlie had brought from Shady Rest through the back clearing to douse out the flames. Everyone gathered together in front of Rose's pretty shaken but proud as peacocks that Clairie's plan had worked.

As we drove back to the farmhouse early that mornin', I remember those bright white, bloodstained sheets lying in the field that the cowards had shed as they ran. We all stared and shook our heads as we drove by realizing just how close we came to disaster. After the display that we had put on, we would never again be bothered by folks like that.

Chapter 6

A few weeks later the Sherriff dropped by to look at the damage and take a report. Pa met him at the road and told him that wouldn't be necessary. We had already started rebuilding and were almost done, so there wasn't really any evidence to look at. That big bull rubbed his belly and told Pa that it was a matter of law and order that he be allowed to see Rose's. Pa stared long and hard at the smirk on top of that badge, and both of them slowly eased a hand toward their pistols.

About then Clairie came out the front door of the farmhouse like the force of nature she was. She was on top of the Sherriff before he could even blink. She bellied right up to that lawman nose to nose and told him she knew two things. Number one was that the real criminals would never be caught, that was a surefire, dead certainty. Number two was that those horse tracks Gus had followed led to a barn that was owned by the one and only, Sherriff himself. The ol' portly fella didn't have much to say about that, but the click of George's unseen rifle told him all he needed to know. He tightened his lip and gave Clairie a good long stare before he let out a huff. Then he looked around, saw Rob and Bats coming down the path from Rose's. He shot Pa a glare that would stop a weak man's heart, but Pa stood straight and glared right back. The defeated knight tipped his hat to Clairie first, then Lily and Rose who had stepped outside on the porch. He gave them a gratuitous "Mam" then the ol' Sherriff got back in his car and headed on down the road. Pa watched all the way til he was out of sight then he turned and told us all, "He won't be Sherriff much longer." He gave us a wink as we all laughed, every one of us standin' there knew Pa was right.

One thing that everyone in Little Egypt knew was that the bootlegging business was booming. The Shelton Brothers and Charlie had their troubles, but they continued to make money no matter how outrageous their feud became. The money rolled in from all different kinds of places. Whiskey from Canada, rum from the Caribbean, gambling machines and of course, houses of pleasure.

There were many dollhouses scattered throughout the countryside in rural Southern Illinois, places like Cactus Patch and Sinkhole. Not far from Rose's, there was an abandoned store that was used as such a place. It was the general store and post office of Foxville, a town that disappeared when the railroad came through. The locals called that old store Stickerbush, and it wasn't pretty on the outside, but on the inside, it was darn fancy. There was a saloon, kitchen, hotel and of course, women for hire. Clairie and Lily had gone to school with the madam of Stickerbush, Ms. Dena. Throughout the years they all remained friends

so my cousins would check in on the place once in a while to make sure that the working girls had everything they needed to be safe. It was a dangerous occupation in those days, but like I said earlier, demand dictates supply.

Clairie and Lily understood that there was a never-ending supply of demand so they tried to help the girls out any way they could. They would bring them clothes, home-cooked meals and hygiene products. They definitely didn't tolerate any man beatin' on the girls either. There was more than one occasion where they would track down some local fella that had taken advantage and introduce him to the muscle of the crew, Rob or their new friend Bats. They also wouldn't tolerate underage girls working there. You see, Ms. Dena didn't own the building or the girls, she was just in charge of the ones they sent her. They would rotate the girls from place to place, and sometimes they would be closer to my age than an adult. That's when Ms. Dena would make a call to Clairie.

When they would get those phone calls my cousins would work with Ms. Dena and plan a whole rescue mission. They would usu-ally leave in the middle of the night and sneak the girls out so as not to be seen by anyone during the jailbreak. They would make sure the girls had a place to go, it usually wasn't their home, but Clairie knew people that would house them for a spell. A few of those girls even stayed at the farmhouse for a night or two before they started a new life somewhere else. Lily had friends in the city that would get them jobs and find them places to live. My cousins took a lot of pride in those daring adventures and risked their own hides many times to give a young girl a new start.

I got to ride along on one of those midnight missions when I accidentally fell asleep in the back of the farm truck. Aunt Rose and I had been out pickin' strawberries all day, so when we got back, I just zonked out. I guess nobody bothered to wake me so when Clairie got a call to come right away, they started the truck up and rolled out with me in the back.

We were almost to Stickerbush before they realized I was an accidental stowaway.

That particular night was when my cousins decided they were

going to use a special weapon that they had been workin' on for a while. I peeked into the cab of the truck, and I could see four big jars in the floorboard by Lily's feet. Those same jars had been sitting outside at the farmhouse for months on end. I never knew what was in em and never asked, but it looked a foul mess. I said a little prayer for whoever was gonna be on the gettin' end of that.

We drove quietly down the little country lane that led up the hill to Stickerbush, and suddenly, Ms. Dena appeared out of the bushes to wave us down. She was dressed as dapper as the devil in a long flowing dress

and store-bought hat. Her long cigarette holder almost hung out over the road as we approached. I could hear the music being played in the saloon and the whole place was lit up and alive. The old store seemed to be bursting with fun, and I couldn't understand what could be so urgently wrong. As I was gettin' a good look at the place, Ms. Dena stepped up on the side rail. She said something to Clairie then turned to me with a surprised look. "Oh, hey handsome!" she whispered with a wink and then disappeared back into the night. Clairie drove up a little further and then she pulled over to the side of the lane about a hundred yards from the house. Lily and she jumped out then told me to turn the truck around and keep it runnin'.

I started to get a little worried while I was spinning the truck around. There were a lot of cars there and if the wrong person noticed one of the girls being snuck out, well no telling what could happen. I could see my cousin's silhouettes drenched in moonlight as they ran right up to the house with those jars in tow. Their shadows stretched long as if they were giants creepin' across the countryside. I lost sight of 'em for a second when the truck stalled, and I had to restart it. When I caught sight of em again, Clairie had climbed up a ladder to the second floor and placed one of those open jars on the window sill. She climbed down, and they went to the other side of the house where I couldn't see what they were doin'. I made sure I was ready to make a clean getaway cuz' I knew what was in them jars.

A few minutes later, everyone found out the answer. The midnight wind was blowin' the scent of that homemade gas all through the house. The first sign of commotion came from upstairs when all of a sudden I could hear a man yellin' and cussin'. Then there were a few more as people started spillin' out every door. They were coughin' and spittin', cussin' and there were a few throwin' up all around the ol' store. This went on for a good while, and I'll admit, I was havin' a pretty good laugh at all those people in chaos.

All the commotion was quite a show, but my fun was interrupted suddenly as Clairie, Lily, Ms. Dena, and a frail, young girl all climbed into the cab of the truck. They frightened me at first because they had warsh rags tied around their faces and clothes pins pinchin' their noses shut. They looked like the strangest bandits you ever seen. I hopped out the driver's seat and into the bed of the truck. Just then did I barely get a whiff of what was in those jars. Oh lord, it was bad, my throat was burnin', and my eyes were waterin' as we sped off down the lane into the night.

I don't think one person saw us as we made our escape. I really felt sorry for those people left behind, that smell was the most awful thing I'd ever come in contact with. I stuck my head in the back window and yelled inappropriately, "What was in those jars?!" Clairie and Lily never flinched, but Ms. Dena turned to me and said smiling, "Oh honey, not now." She put her arm around that thin, young girl who never raised her head. Her hair was matted and greasy, her dress was torn and had dirt ground into it. That moment I realized that I was the only one really having fun that night. There were bigger things going on than loud, raucous saloons and jars with foul smells. I decided I would save my questions for later.

By the time we got back to the farmhouse at Rose's, the young girl had passed out from exhaustion. Clairie carried her inside, and they got to tendin' to her. I sat on the front porch for a while listening to the crickets and the toads. Pretty soon Aunt Rose came out with a lantern in one hand, a bottle in the other. She sat down next to me and forced the wine bottle into my hand. This was not the first time I had tasted Rose's wine, but it was the first time she had offered it to me. After I took a nice healthy sip, Rose said, "You had a rough night huh kiddo?"

Right then I just started cryin', to this day I'm really not sure why but tears just came. After a few minutes and a few wipes of snot on Rose's dress, she spoke again, "You okay?"

I told her I was, but I had to ask, "What was in those jars?"

She just laughed and took the bottle back. "Listen to me," and she sat me up straight so I could look in her eyes. "I'm gonna learn ya somethin'."

She then explained to me exactly what was goin' on with that girl. It was complicated, and it took Aunt Rose a good while to get out what she was tryin' to say. I understood more than she thought I did so I helped ease it along a bit by tellin' her what I could gather from common knowledge. Rose sighed and said, "Thank the Lord." She then told me that the girl's name was Viv, and she was there not of her free will. She had been forced into this by her family, and it was important to get her to a safe place. I grew in years that night. It was a lesson my family taught me not by word of mouth but by silent action. There are certain things that are not tolerated and must be dealt with in a certain way as to not get people upset. That's how people ended up getting killed in times like those. Sometimes you have to use a more…creative way to get things done. That was a great lesson to keep with me for the rest of my days.

CHAPTER 7

I learned a lot of lessons from fighting those battles with my family. We made some enemies during that time, but there were some issues that we wouldn't take a pardon to. That's just the way it was, the law of the land sort of speak. Right was right, and if you didn't know that, well, you were probably wrong. We fought those battles with determination and righteousness, but in the spring of '25, there was an enemy that we couldn't fend off. Mother Nature had something planned that would be bigger trouble than anything Little Egypt or America had ever seen. In fact, the world has never seen anything like it since.

There are some people who call natural disasters "acts of God," but I have to disagree. The 1925 Tri-State tornado was definitely not an "act of God," it was an act of pure evil. Only the devil himself could possibly concoct something so destructive and devastatin'. The tornado that is responsible for the most deaths in U.S. history started in southeast Missouri on the afternoon of March eighteenth. It entered Southern Illinois as it crossed the Mississippi River at Gorham and ripped the river town to shreds, killing thirty-four people. It cut a mile-wide path all the way across Little Egypt and into Indiana. The whole storm system blanketed the sky and turned the clear day darker than night. Hail the size of baseballs rained down on the hills, hollers and coal mines. Spindle storms spun off the main funnel-like fingers and gripped the hearts of communities all over Southern Illinois. Small towns like Parrish ceased to exist after that, they were blown from history's sight. The larger towns, Murphysboro and West Frankfort, were leveled to the ground. There were hardly any buildings left standing and what remained of them burned for days afterward. After the storm passed through, there was a red sky on the horizon, and we watched the night glow orange as my family prepared to help.

Clairie, Lily, and Bernie set out for the storm's aftermath immediately. They left as soon as the strong winds let up. They had all been pacin' and pitchin' with the animals all mornin' as if they knew something was on the way. The rest of us went about our daily routine as we watched the rolling grey clouds grow darker blue and then black as they crept closer. It became apparently clear that we would have to put our business to the side for a while to tend to more important things.

The girls packed up and drove southwest not knowin' what they were headin' towards. They took as many bandages, water and first-aid as they could pack into the farm truck. They drove right into the heart of that red devil sky determined to help as many people as they could. They didn't know it at the time but what they were headed for was far worse than any of us could imagine. The horrors that the girls had to face would change their lives for good.

The rest of us packed up the Ford with first-aid supplies, and Pa drove the tractor as we started south. We weren't sure where we were headed, but we knew that help was needed. You could smell the dust and ash in the air as we drove through the night towards Hamilton county. We ended up in Olga, south of Mcleansboro near Dale. You could see the path that wreckin' ball had made through the woods. There were zero trees left standing, and the ones that were left upright were bent ninety degrees. We found a couple of farms where every building was leveled, and we weren't quite sure if there were survivors. There wasn't anyone around, hell there wasn't even animals around, it was just silent. Deathly silent.

We first saw the body as we were drivin' to the second farm we came upon. He was just lyin' out in the middle of a muddy field. Gus stopped the car, but Pa said to drive on up to the house first and see if there were survivors. As we drove down the lane, we could see movement inside the farmhouse that was barely standin'. As we killed the engines, we saw a young man run out the back door of the house. Pa jumped off the tractor and aimed his shotgun at the front door. He had seen there was one more person inside, so he was gonna let that one boy run to keep whoever it was inside under the gun. Pa walked up slowly and shouted gruffly, "Come on out! We got more bullets out here than you do!"

A young boy about my age slowly and sheepishly crept out the front door. He held a small bag in his hands that he let fall to the ground when he saw all those gun barrels starin' at him. Pa lowered his gun and waved at Gus to do the same. He asked the boy, "What's in the bag?" The boy told him it was food. Pa then asked if there was anyone else left in the house and the boy told him no. He then explained that his brother, the one who had run off, and he had been hungry even before the storm. They saw the storm as a way to get some food if there was any left after the wind stopped. They had survived the night hunkered down in a cave that was nearby. After the storm blew through, they went searchin' and ended up at the shell of this house. The boy said he knew nothing about the body in the field. Pa told him, "Take your bag and get! Go catch up to your brother!" The boy was gone in a flash and let out across the field following the same muddy prints his brother had left.

We all took a good look around to see if there were any more surprises hidin' in the rubble. The only building left standin' was the lower half of the farmhouse. It looked like it had been sliced in half by the Reaper himself. The force of the winds had taken down the barn, chicken coup, outhouse, everything was leveled, and the debris was scattered for hundreds of yards all across the fields. We put the farmer's body in the scoop of the tractor and drove into the town of Dale. We hoped someone there could identify him and sure enough, they did. His wife and kids had escaped north of the storm, but the farmer had stayed behind to save what he could. He saved nothing and lost only his life trying to fight a force greater than anything he could have imagined.

Storms like that monster only happen when the perfect conditions occur. The right amount of high pressure, low pressure, moisture in the air and you got yourself a mighty big problem. This devil used all the right ingredients and mixed 'em with the perfect time of day to deal out some real heartache. There were no sirens back then, folks were just going about their daily duties when that ol' wind started windin' up. Mothers were feedin' their babies, farmers were behind their plows, fathers were earnin' their checks and kids were learnin' their lessons in school.

There were several schools that were hit with the full force of the big blow with teachers and children huddled inside. Clairie, Lily, and Bernie, unfortunately, came upon one such aftermath, a sight more horrifying than anything we discovered. They ended up in DeSoto where a whole school was leveled, and thirty-three children were killed. There were also two schools in Murphysboro that were caught dead to rights in the line of destruction. There is nothing more damaging to a community than to lose members of the younger generation, and those communities lost several to one storm.

The girls were there for weeks helpin' recovery and cleanup. They focused on consoling the parents of the lost children and worked right alongside people from all over the country who came to help. They lent their shoulders for cryin', cooked meals for the cleanup crew and delivered first-aid to those they could. Over the years I've tried not to think about what the girls went through. I've tried not to think about what they saw, but those thoughts have crept in. I saw similar destruction in Europe in the second war, but I never had to pull out children from burning rubble. It took a special kind of toughness to do that and then to live with the memories afterward.

I remember the day the girls came back home, it was as if they had been in the trenches of Europe. They had the thousand-yard stare I had seen in soldier's eyes after the first war. At the time, I had no idea what that stare meant but another conflict in Europe years later would show me. The girls reminded me of some of the survivors of that second war, they were pale white from malnourishment and dehydration. Their clothes were ripped and stained with ash. They looked like three ghosts when they walked in the house.

After they cleaned up and had rested a good spell, the girls told us about some of the recovery effort. They had unloaded most of the water in the tiny village of Bush. That evil monster flung boards from the houses it ripped to pieces straight into the water tower. They helped dig people out of the remains that were half alive, and some of them were scorched beyond recognition. Bernie could hardly tell us any details through her tears, and Lily hardly said a peep. Clairie said that the cleanup would go on for months, but they had to leave. She told us that the National

Guard had been instructed to shoot looters on sight and that they had been there when one such looter was gunned down. The strain was too much for them, so they came back home to Marion County.

The Sunday after we all made it back, our neighbors held a pot luck at the farmhouse. Mrs. Lisenby made her famous apple and peach cobbler which was a favorite of our family's. We tried to get things back to normal again, but that's the thing about unexpected disasters. You can put all the trinkets and bottles back on the shelves but somehow it's not the same, it's never the same. That storm not only changed my family, it changed how the whole country looked at the weather. The loss that Little Egypt had to suffer that spring only made the community stronger and better able to handle the storms that were to come.

Chapter 8

The next time we all headed south, it was for a much different reason. The whole family was invited by Charlie to come visit his infamous roadhouse in Williamson County. In between court cases and battlin' the Sheltons, Charlie had managed to build himself a place of his own just on the other side of the Saline county line. He still had some politicians in his pocket in Williamson County, so he was free to run his business as he pleased. Shady Rest quickly became a very popular place and had a little bit of somethin' for everybody.

The BBQ stand had food, soda, beer and if you needed somethin' stronger, you could ask. After hours there was music, and you could gamble on cards in the roadhouse if that was your thrill. There were other things you could bet on if blood was your game, out back there were dog and cockfights.

Charlie had made his own little oasis right there in Little Egypt and sorta like Rose, he had worn out his welcome in some parts. At Shady Rest, Charlie could do what he wanted without the law or the Sheltons breathin' down his neck. They were still his partners, but his trust for the brothers was wearin' thin. He had plenty of fun things to do at Shady, and once in a while, there was live music. He would bring in musicians from all over, even St. Louis. A lot of places wouldn't allow black musicians, but Charlie had no qualms about it. You could see real, authentic blues played at Shady. A couple of times he asked Pa to play, and when Gypsy Jack played, he set fire to the place. The liquor flowed a little more, and the crowd danced, hooted and hollered a little louder.

During those nights when the sun went down, and the bottles were uncorked, I was forced out to the BBQ stand with ol' man Harlow. He was a crazy old timer that ran the stand sometimes. That ol' drunk would start preachin' about some weird cult of Saturn he was scared of, and I would get out the door quick. My gypsy blood doesn't take to that sittin' around so I'd wander around the property on my own free will. I got to learn the lay of the land pretty good, heck, I knew Shady better than some of Charlie's fellow criminals. I snuck around there late at night and never once got caught…well, that's not exactly true.

I got to know a very special friend at Shady during that time. I became friends with Charlie's pet monkey Jocko, who was supposed to stay in the BBQ stand also. He would follow me around some nights as I wandered around in the shadows. He was smart as a whip, maybe even more than some of the people I met at Charlie's hangout. Years later, I would learn that the story of Charlie's downfall had something to do with Jocko. Together we heard all kinds of nonsense as we bounced around the different groups of people that gathered at Shady. There was one night that both of us almost got my family into one heck of a mess.

It was a sticky summer night just after a rainstorm when a fella from out of town brought his dogs to do some fightin'. He had two truckloads of 'em and was determined to lay some money down. Well, on this night that was a problem, Charlie granted my family one exception when we came to Shady. There would be no animal fightin' what so ever while Clairie and Lily were visitin'. It was the only way that Lily would come with us and Charlie would do whatever it took to spend time with Clairie.

No one ever spoke up about it although when I was sneakin' around in the shadows, I did hear a lot of people bad mouth my family because of it. Well, Charlie's boys told this fella they weren't fightin' no dogs that night and boy did he get angry. He called Charlie out as a no good hustler and cursed my family name. He told his buddies that my family was no good gypsy witches and probably had Charlie under some kind of voodoo spell. Well, I just happen to be lurkin' around with Jocko when this ol' boy was jawjackin' so I thought I would let Clairie know what he thought of the Little Roses. I headed toward the roadhouse, but that loudmouth happened to see Jocko and I as we went in between the trees. He called us out and yelled at a couple of his fellas to run over and snatch me and Jocko from our hidin' spot. They dragged us out into the firelight, and that ramblin' fool hollered out.

"Well lookie here! It's that witch's boy and a gol' darn chimp!"

The group of 'em laughed it up as Jocko, and I squirmed tryin' to get away. The next thing that 'ol boy had to say sealed his fate. "If we can't fight no dogs, maybe we can fight these two!"

Most of the crowd roared and jeered but I saw a few younger boys take off up the path to the roadhouse. I knew where they were headin', so I told that feller to "Get bent!" He didn't take so kindly to me mouthin', him, so he pushed me into the crowd then grabbed Jocko and hoisted him in the air. That monkey could be mean when he wanted, and he connected with a right hook to that guy's temple. The crowd got riled up, shufflin' me amongst themselves as Jocko and that fool tussled in the dirt. The fella finally got a hold of Jocko and tossed him into the crowd also. Those fools were upsettin' him somethin' fierce as they passed him roughly from man to man.

The unfortunate fella from out of town was right in the middle of it with his buddies as Clairie, and the group from the roadhouse approached. He said real loud, "Now what does this little girl want." I reckon that was the last thing he said for a few weeks. Clairie didn't say a word, never broke stride and quickly walked up swinging. He turned around just as she put every ounce of her anger into his face. She broke that fella's jaw and stunned everyone standing there. It sounded like Hornsby hittin' the sweet spot when her fist landed on his jaw. They both hit the dirt, and before anyone could even blink, Clairie had picked herself up, brushed the dirt off and shot them other boys a glare that would stop a clock.

There was a tense moment as both groups just stared at each other. One side in stunned silence and the other in quiet rage. The silence was broken by that familiar click of George's rifle and then a loud groan as the broke gambler picked himself up off the ground. He couldn't quite get to his feet and fell right back in the dust with another yellowed cowl. The out of towners quickly realized that they were outnumbered, outgunned and had just learned a hard lesson. Do not mess with the ladies, especially if they have the last name Rose. They threw up their hands and told everyone they would take their dogs and leave, which they quickly did.

After those ramblin' fools had left, the parade of people that walked back up to the roadhouse were already retelling the story. They were givin' Clairie draws off their flasks and slappin' her on the back like she was one of the boys. I actually got to hang out in the roadhouse that night, and I'll never forget the smells when I first walked in, they were very familiar to me. A cloud of tobacco smoke and a whiff of Pa's liquor made me feel right at home.

Charlie's place was cozy on the inside with deer's antlers' on the wall around the bar and a huge stone fireplace. The people at Shady that night were fired up from the excitement so if you were there, you darn sure remembered it.

I got to see Pa play the guitar with Polly, the fiddle player he played with when he was at Shady. The crowd sure did love them, I remember lookin' around the room and only seeing smiles as they spilled so much liquor on the dance floor that everybody's shoes were soaked by the time they left. Aunt Rose even sang a couple of tunes, and the girls danced while everyone sang along with her. I got to see a glimpse of a very special performance that evening by a Southern Illinois legend. A woman who they called the Blonde Bombshell got up to dance while Pa was playin' and that was about the time that Clairie and Lily escorted me to the door. She was a fan favorite at Shady Rest, but I was a few years away from being allowed to watch her dance

After they shoved me out the door, I stood on the porch for a moment before I realized I was not alone. In the shadows, there was a woman smoking a cigarette and sippin' on a glass of whiskey. She called out to me with a whisper, "Psst, hey kid, what's your name?" I told her it was Owen and she recognized me as Gypsy Jack's boy. "Your Pa makes the finest whiskey around here. Even better than you can get in the city."

I told her "Thanks" and shyly looked away. She stood up and revealed her beauty to me in the moonlight.

"My name is Helen." then she held out her gloved hand. I was so nervous I thought I might wet my trousers, but I reached out and kissed her hand as I thought a gentleman might. About that time the door swung open and out stepped big Carl Shelton. Well the sight of him just made me more nervous, so I quickly disappeared into the shadows as they sped off in his car.

I had some very good memories from my time at Charlie's hideout, but many folks didn't. There were some that didn't get to tell their story, and there were others who died because they did. It was easy for trouble to find you at Shady Rest even if you weren't lookin' for it. Charlie found himself in a whole lot of trouble in the next few months so it would be a little while before we visited his place again. Pa said it was best if we stayed to ourselves during that time because the Birger gang was about to be in real hot water. Pa wasn't lying, the law came down hard on Charlie and the Sheltons over the next few years. Southern Illinois residents were startin' to get their fill of the robberies and killin' that took place between the rivers. Justice would come callin' for some, and others had a different kind of reckoning come knockin' at their door.

CHAPTER 9

The heavy hand of the law would finally start to catch up to Charlie and the Sheltons when bodies started piling up. The rivals had teamed up to fend off the KKK once again and had dispatched of the menace that was S. Glenn Young. We tried to keep up with all the news in the local papers, but it was confusin', to say the least. There were some strange bedfellows during that time, and it was hard to know who was on who's side and who was dead or alive. Soon it would become clear that there was a split between the gangsters as both were going to extreme measures to destroy the other. They each had armored vehicles built to protect themselves from the onslaught of bullets they had to dodge. They would drive them through towns to show them off and to intimidate their rivals.

The Shelton brothers even made history when they decided to attack Charlie's oasis in Williamson county from a different angle. They hired a local crop duster and flew over Shady Rest droppin' dynamite right onto the property. They didn't do much damage, but that was the lengths the rum runners were willing to go to put Charlie and his gang out of business. Soon after the bombin' we were lookin' to put an end to Charlie for a reason that had nothin' to do with business. Our reason was personal, and it would be the beginning of the end to my family's way of life.

During the fall in Southern Illinois before the leaves die off the branches, the trees turn all kinds of beautiful colors. Crimson reds, canary yellows and bright oranges are all you can see as you drive through the countryside. It's really my favorite time of year to live in Little Egypt. The autumn wind always reminds me that the good times don't always last. Our family had been reaping the benefits of our business for quite a few years by then so it was about time the cold wind blew our way.

The farmers were reaping their minimal harvests that year, and a community tradition back then was to have a picnic at the Little Prairie school to celebrate another year of crops. Everyone was invited, and the women kept the pots full all, day, so when the threshers came in, they could eat too. It was sort of a Thanksgiving celebration with the whole town instead of just our little family. We would drag the tables and chairs out of the school into the yard so we could all eat together. Everyone would bring their special dish and the whole afternoon would be filled with food, music and games.

I remember runnin' through the yard chasin' that Lisenby girl when I saw Charlie's Lincoln and another car comin' down the road. None of us knew that he was gonna be joinin' us that afternoon, so it was a surprise when two carloads of gangsters pulled up. We didn't have any problems with Charlie, but he made people in the community a bit nervous when he came around. They had read the papers and heard the stories of all the things Charlie had been accused of. Yet there he was,

free as a bird on the wind in a fancy auto that looked brand new. Connie was in a car behind him, and it didn't take a genius to figure out why he had come along. My first thought was that there could be trouble because Gus was there and that could cause some tension. Lily knew what to do to ease that though, she walked right up to Connie and told him not to start any nonsense. He promised he wouldn't and ended up sharing his flask with Gus who normally didn't drink liquor.

That was just one of the unusual events that occurred as the afternoon faded into evening. The picnic was the same as every year, the kids ran and yelled while the adults played horseshoes and cards while bottles were passed around. The sun was startin' to set when Charlie, Clairie, and Pa went inside the school to talk business. A few minutes later we could hear voices start to raise a little. Most of the folks had left, but the ones that remained began to pack up the rest of the picnic as the argument only got worse. They had always seen eye to eye so none of us could believe how bad the yellin' got. The next thing we heard was a desk overturned then the door come flyin' open, and Charlie came out cussin'. He made a b-line for his Lincoln and roared out of the driveway stoppin' only long enough for a couple of his henchmen to hop in. Clairie and Pa just shook their heads as they watched Charlie roll on down the road. There had been some talk of the price of Gypsy Jack's and considerin' that Charlie was scramblin' for money, well that sorta tells the story, doesn't it?

A few minutes after Charlie tore off in his new Lincoln. Connie and the remaining crew of gangsters piled into the Chrysler and hit the road also. Connie had his fill of watching Gus and Lily have a good time, so he headed back down south. That flask he was passin' around sure did a number on Gus. He was way too drunk to get behind the wheel, so Lily drove, and as she waved goodbye, the sun dipped below the horizon.

The rest of us packed up the leftovers and put the chairs back inside the schoolhouse. Mrs. Hickey held our family dear, so she gave us all big hugs before we left any gatherins'. When she gave Clairie a hug, she paused a moment and squeezed her again. She grabbed her shoulders and told her that the second one was for Lily since she had left in such a rush. I noticed the look on Clairie's face when Mrs. Hickey gave her that second hug, and I'll never forget the chill that ran up my spine. Her expression suddenly became pale despair, and she thanked Mrs. Hickey, then hurried us all into the car. Clairie drove as we flew down the county line heading straight into the darkness that awaited.

That coupe had been on many a midnight run, but I don't think that Ford was ever driven faster than it was that night. There were two blood red taillights starin' at us as we came up over the hill. Clairie muttered "I knew it" out loud as she stomped on the gas. Aunt Rose and I were in the back when she reached over, grabbed my hand and squeezed. Pa jumped out before the car even stopped movin' and ran to the driver's door of the car in the ditch. When he got there, he froze in his tracks and then just hung his head as he collapsed to his knees. Clairie opened the car door and pulled Lily's limp body from the wreckage. Aunt Rose and I watched in silence as this morbid scene played out in front of us. I have dreamt about that moment thousands of times, Clairie pulling Lily out of the car. It is a haunting memory that reminds me of the worst day of my life and an end to the life we knew.

At some point during the tears and the chaos, we realized that Gus was still alive lying in the ditch. He was battered and bloody, but he was breathing. Aunt Rose and I got him in the car then drove to the nearest farmhouse to call the doc. Ol' man Halfacre let us use his phone, so we told the Doc where Lily was then went to cleanin' and bandagin' up Gus's wounds. He had a broken arm and a real good shiner from a direct hit to his temple. He told us he couldn't remember exactly what, happened, but he was sure he had seen a car come out of nowhere right before they hit the ditch. He thought maybe he had heard a gunshot as the car went past, but he wasn't sure. We decided to let him rest, so we laid him up and went to tell Pa and Clairie what we had learned from Gus.

As we arrived back on the scene, we could see that Doc was tendin' to Lily. Clairie stood over them crying, her dress soaked with blood. We walked over to where Pa was standing with the rest of the family. Everyone was huggin' and prayin', cryin' and hopin' that somehow our darling Lily would pull through. Clairie and Doc stayed with her until the coroner arrived and when he pulled out his sheets, we knew that it was over. The heart of our family sank into our guts all at once. Standing in the dark that night, we watched the shine from our jewel of Little Egypt go permanently dim.

CHAPTER 10

Later that evening as we sat around Rose's stunned there was a lot of fuss about who was responsible and what to do about Lily's death. We knew that it had to be one of two cars that could have caused the wreck and both had the motivation to cause some damage. The coupe had definitely been shot at, we found a bullet lodged in the door frame of the car, but Lily's injuries didn't show a gunshot wound. The mystery car had run Lily and Gus off the road as it drove by to fire a warning shot or trying to dodge the bullet Lily lost control of the wheel. Either way, there was just cause for retribution, but the family was split on who they thought the guilty party was. Clairie was convinced that it was Connie, she thought that he had finally gotten fed up with playin' second fiddle to Gus. She figured that Connie would have thought Gus was drivin', but Lily was, so he didn't know he was actually shootin' at her instead of his intended target.

Pa and the boys thought that it was Charlie who did the shootin'. He was mad about money plus he had other troubles down south that only doubled his anxiety. They knew that Charlie had no problem with taking revenge by using a gun and maybe he had just thought a warning shot would help Pa and Clairie change their mind about that price of Gypsy Jack's. That reasoning did make some sense, so it was possible that a bullet fired from Charlie's pistol had caused Lily to drive off the road and the impact caused her injuries. Aunt Rose was three sheets to the wind and was inconsolable, so the argument went on and on well past midnight as every candle in the place burned down to the hilt.

A decision was finally made to wait until after the funeral to make any kind of plans for revenge. For days after the crash, a dark cloud hung over Rose's like a thick, confusing fog. We were all still in shock and time seemed to stand still for a while. Clairie was the only one who seemed to be able to keep her wits about her although everyone treated her like an open knife. She was the one that suggested we wait and keep our ears to the wind. We were bound to hear something, she told us that eventually, the truth would come out in the wash. We didn't have a lot of clues, and Gus had little memory as to who had shot at the car. He was stone drunk when it happened and had a serious head injury to boot. There was one person who we wouldn't hear from until he surprisingly showed up at Lily's funeral.

Connie was there to pay his respect and boy did Clairie glaze him with hellfire right there in front of everyone. Brother Riley and Pa tried to calm her down, but it was no use. She wouldn't let Connie even explain his side of the story. She just yelled at him through her tears, but I had a feeling there was some truth to what Connie was tryin' to say. I knew that if he had done the shootin', he wouldn't dare show his face around our family no more. He would have tucked tail and run if he was truly guilty. Aunt Rose was so upset she didn't even show up. She had taken off on a bender, and we hadn't seen her since the morning after the wreck.

After the funeral Connie and Pa had a long talk as soon as Clairie had driven off. Connie explained that he hadn't even gone down the county line the night of the crash. He had gone straight south instead of going east toward Rose's. He suspected that Charlie had gone that way for the sole purpose of causin' some kind of havoc. Connie swore with tears in his eyes that he had no knowledge of how it happened. When he found out that Lily had died in the crash, he had confronted and almost killed Charlie over the whole ordeal.

I don't believe that Connie Newman was a bad man, but he took orders from one and that there says a lot. The web that surrounded Charlie was a tangled one, and a lot of people who didn't deserve an early grave found themselves buried six feet in the ground.

One of Charlie's victims turned out to be a huge help in the search for Lily's killer. During the next few weeks, we heard stories from everyone we knew, but the talk at the local roadhouses was all speculation and hearsay. There was no shred of solid evi-

dence until we got a visit from an Illinois State Policeman who had got word to Pa that he had inside information.

He set up a meeting at Rose's late one winter night. I remember he came on horseback through the woods, careful not to be seen. He only talked to Pa and Clairie in the back bar, but I managed to sneak into a spot where I could eavesdrop on the conversation. The policeman told them that he ran a car thievin' scam with Charlie and hung out at Shady Rest a lot. He had overheard some of the gangsters talkin' about the wreck that killed Lily. He said that Charlie had been stompin' mad with Pa and Clairie, so he waited for them on the county line. When Lily passed Charlie, blinded by rage, he overtook the coupe and fired a shot at the driver side window. The bullet had hit the door frame but scared Lily so much that she lost control of the vehicle and slammed into the ditch. Charlie and his gangsters just kept on drivin', not caring who lived or died. He said that Connie had nothin' to do with it and he was mad at Charlie for killin' the girl he was sweet on. Pa and Clairie didn't say much to the man. They thanked him for tellin' what he had heard and gave him a bottle for his honesty. With this new information, Clairie was ready to head south and find Charlie, but Pa told her he had been hearin' things that just might change her mind.

Charlie's webs were starting to unravel one by one, and he was makin' enemies he didn't even know he had. Pa thought it was only a matter of time before the law would lock Charlie up and turned out he was right. Lily was not Charlie's only victim that winter, the mayor of West City had been murdered in his own home. Two gunmen, who most people thought were hired by Charlie, knocked on his door, gave him a handwritten note and shot him dead. Eventually, that would be the crime that Charlie Birger would famously hang for. Not long after the mayor's murder, that state policeman who had offered up his secrets to us disappeared. His wife vanished along with him, a local schoolteacher who was rumored to be pregnant. Half the state of Illinois was lookin' for her, and after what seemed like a never-ending search that went on for weeks, she was eventually found in an abandoned mine shaft. Almost everyone that knew the story thought Charlie was responsible for all these crimes.

Before they could throw him in jail, the gangster's oasis in Williamson county was burned to the ground. A lot of people that knew our family thought for sure that we had something to do with it. Rose and Clairie were both known for their tendency to say "Gonna set a fire!" but I can tell ya for sure that I was with Clairie all night when Shady Rest burned.

The real culprit remains a mystery to this day with some believing that it was the Sheltons or members of Birger's own gang who had issues with Charlie. There were scorched bodies found inside, and some still believe that the gangster himself lit the match. I'd say by now there's no one alive who knows the real story so we will never know the truth.

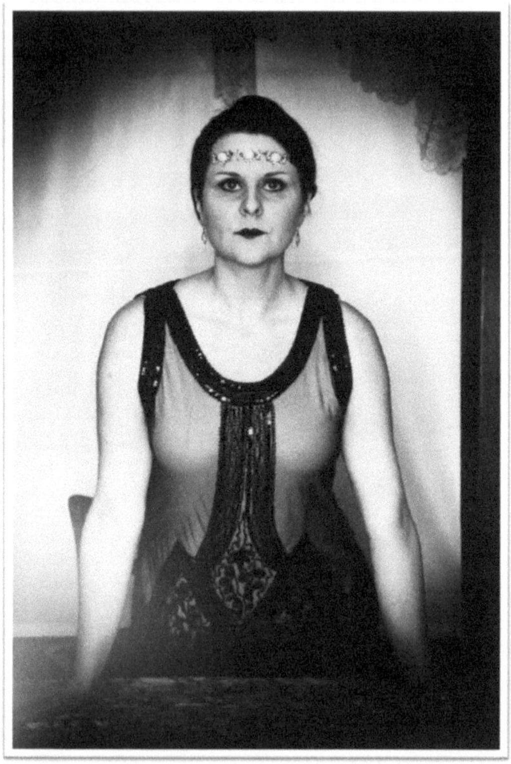

The public would learn the truth about the murders soon enough. The brothers that killed the mayor confessed and told authorities that Charlie had hired them to shoot Joe Adams. In June of '27 Charlie was arrested and sent to jail in Franklin County. When

Clairie found that out, she tried more than once to get inside that jail, but Charlie was heavily guarded and even got to keep his Tommy gun in the cell with him. The trial was in the papers from coast to coast every day, and the courtroom was packed to the rafters. Eventually, Charlie was found guilty, and he was to be hung by the neck until dead, dead, dead in April of 1928.

The night before Charlie's last day we drove overnight through Jefferson County and into Benton. We spent the night at Doc Alvis's house so we could get up early and make sure to get a good viewing spot. We all wanted to get a good look at the last moments of our ol' friend. It was a beautiful sunny day, and you could smell the fresh blossoms poppin' in the air. People from every nook and cranny of Little Egypt and all over the country came to watch. The town square was overflowing with folks from every walk of life. There were reporters from towns I'd never heard of. There were lawmen, lawbreakers, victims of Charlie's crimes and some perpetrators of 'em too. The rooftops were filled, and the crowd was thick as molasses. Pa and I got as close as we could, but Clairie pushed her way to the front, and told everyone who could hear, "I'd kill him myself if he wasn't fixin' to swing." She wanted to see him eye to eye one more time before he was sent off to the afterlife.

Pa had managed to step up onto some steps and hoisted me onto his shoulders as the time of death drew nearer. I seem to remember time slowing down as Charlie was brought out and marched to the giant wooden gallows built just for the hangin'. He had a smile on his face and even greeted a few of the people he knew as he was escorted to the steps. He shuddered a little as he walked by Clairie, but she never said a word or flinched. She just stared him down, and for a moment I thought she might go for his throat herself. But she didn't, she showed restraint knowing that in a few moments the noose would bear the weight of her grief and sorrow.

There were quiet whispers that made their way through the crowd as to what Charlie was sayin'. He had chosen a black hood over white 'cuz accordin' to the whispers Charlie said, "I never liked the colors of the Klux." Those closest to the gallows would write that his last words were "It's a beautiful world." but the whispers told us he said, "It's a beautiful day." On either account, Charlie was right. To most people at the Franklin County jail that day, it was a beautiful day, and the world was going to be more beautiful without the murderous gangster around.

As they were fittin' the noose, I saw some boys climb up a tree to get a better look. I wanted to join 'em, but there was no gettin' over there in time before the rope snapped. I felt sad for Charlie, he had always been nice to me, gave me free soda pop at the BBQ stand. He always had a story to tell me about when he was my age slingin' newspapers in the streets of St. Louis. He had been sweet on Clairie for years, and my family shared many laughs with him.

In the end, he let his anger get the best of him, and that was the reason for a lot of the violence during that time. Anger is a lot like whiskey, it can be a real devil sometimes.

Chapter 11

Many more criminals from the Birger gang would be put on trial and sentenced to life in prison or death. One of them being Connie Newman who I heard years later died in prison. As far as the Little Rose family goes, Lily's death was the end of our little business. Aunt Rose was hardly around anymore, she stayed in the roadhouses that littered the countryside. Pa made liquor, but he only kept one still. Gypsy Jack's would fade into the dark closets of history because he only made small batches for himself and a little for a few friends. I would stay out there with him most nights because the farmhouse and Rose's sat empty most of the time.

Over the years the weeds grew up, and the porch roof began to sag a little. It was just a sad reminder of a happier time for all of us, so we didn't really want to be there. Pa and I had that gypsy blood in us, so we moved around a lot, lived off the land. When Pa needed more whiskey, we would head back to the still. It was hard times, but I didn't mind being a wanderer, I kinda came to like it in the end.

When the twenties came to an end, Pa bought a small farmhouse further down the county line towards Papertown. It sat on eighty acres with a barn, cattle pond and a brand new chicken coup. There was one piece missin' though.

The night after Charlie was hung, Clairie packed her bags in the coupe and sat down with us to say goodbye. A piece of her had died when Lily did, and I don't think there was anything that could ease that pain. She told us that she couldn't live one more day in Little Egypt without her sister. She didn't want to drink herself

into an early grave like Rose, and she couldn't just live with the ghosts like Pa and me. She chose to run, and I don't think she ever stopped once she left. We understood and tried not to cry too much as she said her final good-bye. Before she walked out the door, she handed me a leather bound journal with a small leather strap around it. She told me she was finished with that one and had started a new one.

I had no idea what she was givin' me at the time, but she handed over all the family secrets that she knew. She split up some money with Pa, packed up as much Gypsy Jack's as she could and drove off into the night. We never heard from her again and honestly, not one member of our family ever tried to search for her. We knew that it would be of no use. She disappeared out of history, but she left a deep impact on me. I always took on my problems head-on and with vigor just like she did. It served me well in the war and most times in life.

I've kept that ol' journal all these years, and when Rose's started fallin' down, I took the pictures off the walls. I tucked the pictures you see in this book on the inside of that journal, and there they stayed for decades. No one ever saw them but me, maybe my wife once or twice. On nights when I've had a glass or two of Rose's homemade wine (I kept the recipe close to my heart), I pull those pictures out and think about the good times. I try not to think of Lily's death, but eventually, my thoughts end up there. In my later years, I learned to grow award-winning flowers, and my Lily's always took first place.

After the second world war, I came back to Southern Illinois and lived on the farm with Pa for a few years. Once in a while, I would attend services at Donoho Prairie Church. I found religion during the war real quick, as most men did. I went to grade school with the preacher, and I knew most of the folk that went there. One sunny Sunday I saw a new face in the crowd that was millin' about after the preacher had let us go. There was a pretty girl that looked familiar to me, and when I caught her eye, she walked right up to me and asked if I remembered her. Well, I had to embarrassingly admit that I didn't. She told me that her name was Viv and my cousins had rescued her from Stickerbush when she was a young girl.

I couldn't believe my eyes or ears, but there she was, flesh and blood, pretty as a picture. She told me that a large family that lived nearby had taken her in as their own. She grew up in the area although our paths had never crossed over the years. Probably because I didn't really go to regular school and I was never in one place for very long. The next

Sunday I kindly asked her out on a date. She accepted and around a year later we got married. Sometimes, the plan is way bigger than you could ever imagine.

Viv and I raised three kids, Jack, Rose and Lily. They all have families of their own, and when Jack's first daughter was born, he named her Clairie. As the kids got older, they wanted to know what happened to the older Clairie. They said that with the internet and DNA it would be easy to find her. I wasn't so sure that they could find her and really didn't think they would. They started to search, and it took 'em quite a few months. They traced a trail that zigzagged all over the country, but they eventually found her in Jacksonville, Florida. She lived under one assumed name after another as she ran from her past until she was too old to get around. She retired to a beach house and had passed away many years before they knew who she was. I wasn't sure all their information was correct, but there was one interesting clue that left no doubt in my mind that it was Clairie. When the assumed woman died and they cleared out her house, in the very back of one of her cabinets was a jar colored golden amber. On the top of that jar in old cursive was a homemade label that read in faded ink, "Gypsy Jack's 1928."

Pa passed on in '74, we aren't sure, but he was over a hundred when he died. I still have his hat, his pipe and of course his famous recipe that has never been written down. I like to make a small batch now and then. I'll sit on the porch late at night, close my eyes and go back to my childhood. Somewhere off in the distance, I can hear the crack of a rifle as the boys shoot some target practice. I can smell the blossoms from Rose's orchard and see her dancin' in between the trees. I can smell Pa's beard, forever stained with tobacco smoke from his pipe. I can hear Clairie and Lily laughin', carryin' on inside the roadhouse. Their voices echoing through the still night. I can taste the sweet, golden whiskey that warms your whole spirit as it goes down. Mainly and most importantly, I can feel the love that held my family together during all kinds of hard times. Nothing beats that feeling, nothing in the world. There are folks that to this day think that my family was just a bunch of criminals. That's fine with me, let them think what they want. I'm not one to be a braggart or tell tall tales but if you wanna call me a name, then call me one I'm proud of. A bootlegger.

The End

About the Artists

Growing up in the small village of Kell in Southern Illinois, Brian showed an interest in the arts at an early age. His first query into expression came in the form of writing. Eventually turning those words into song lyrics, he became the front man for a small, successful touring band.

After a decade of writing short stories and poetry, Brian's first publication came in a local magazine and later he self-published a short story teaming up with photographer Robbie Edwards. Partners in art and life, they reside in Southern Illinois and continue to progress as artists together.

Robbie Edwards is a vintage inspired photographer self-taught through constant experimentation. Using her dreams as inspiration she re-creates them, bringing to life her inner fantasies. Balancing the challenges of motherhood and progressive art, she continues to build strength in both mediums.

We would like to thank the following people for helping us see this dream to the end:

Our wonderful cast who we think of as family now. You were all patient, cooperative and surprised us by your dedication and talent.

Owen Braden- Owen Monroe

Eastwood Frisch- Gypsy Jack

Sherry Williams- Rose

Laura Husk- Clairie

Dena Kabat- Ms. Dena

Josh Nelson- Gus

George Williams- George

Matt Loucks- Bats

Lauren Schaubert- Lily   **Maggie Sanders- Viv**

William Garretson- Charlie Birger   **Rob Whisenhunt- Rob**

Eric Gockel- Connie Newman   **Rachel Hunsell- Bernice**

Special thanks to Mike Ogle for his portrayal of Brother Riley and for putting his own special touch to our project.

Mr. Marvin and Vivian Scott for the use of their feed store as our first location. We had a wonderful time learning the history of your place.

The family of Cady Bayler, her father Vince Ragan for the use of his Ford coupe and Mr. Ed and Donna Betts for the use of their cabins. A beautiful car and perfect location for our shoot. You treated us like family and our whole cast had a great time exploring your place.

Russell Brown from the Granada Theatre in downtown Mt. Vernon for letting us turn your bar into Shady Rest for an afternoon. You are always gracious to our creative endeavors.

Tracy Webb from Rend Lake College Theater Department for wardrobe, props and her expertise. We look forward to working with you again in the future. Staley sends a special thanks to Josie for being so nice.

Krissy Clark Braden for your dedication to our project and supplying wardrobe for Owen.

Finally, all the staff at Words Matter Publishing who made our first experience with a publishing house a pleasant one. Very special thanks to Tammy Koelling for her patience and the willingness to take a chance on two small town kids with big dreams.

I would like to thank the authors of the following sources for their dedication to the history of Little Egypt. I was easily projected back in time by your thorough account of the events during prohibition in Southern Illinois.

Gary Williams for the use of your Grandparent's house for our last shoot. The spring flowers made the perfect setting for our finale.

Books

Angle, Paul M. *Bloody Williamson*. New York: Alfred A. Knopf, 1952.

Bain, Donald. *Charlie and the Shawneetown Dame*. Johnson City: A.E.R.P, 1978.

DeNeal, Gary. *A Knight of Another Sort: Prohibition Days and Charlie Birger*. Carbondale: Southern Illinois University Press, 1998.

Erwin, Milo and Jon Musgrave. *The Bloody Vendetta of Southern Illinois*. Marion: IllinoisHistory.com, 2006

Pensoneau, Taylor. *Brothers Notorious: The Sheltons*. New Berlin: Downstate Publications, 2002.

Website
www.wchis.org